HOW THE TWO IVANS QUARRELLED

BY

NIKOLAI GOGOL

British Library Cataloguing-in-Publication Data
A catalogue record for this book is available from the
British Library

Contents

Nikolai Gogol

Nikolai Vasilievich Gogol was born in Sorochintsi, Ukraine in 1809. He attended the Poltava boarding school, and then the Nehzin high school, where he wrote for the school's literary journal and acted in theatrical productions. In 1828, after leaving school, Gogol moved to St. Petersburg with the ambition of becoming a professional author. At his own expense, he published a long Romantic poem. It was universally derided, and Gogol bought and destroyed all the copies, swearing never to write poetry again.

In 1831, Gogol brought out the first volume of his Ukrainian stories, *Evenings on a Farm Near Dikanka*. It met with immediate success, and he followed it a year later with a second volume. Around this time, Gogol met the great Russian poet Aleksandr Pushkin, with whom he developed a close friendship. Over the next decade or so, he worked with great industry, producing a great amount of short stories. Of these, 'The Nose' is regarded as a masterwork of comic short fiction, and 'The Overcoat' is now seen as one of the greatest short stories ever written; some years later, Dostoyevsky famously stated "We all come out from Gogol's 'Overcoat'." He also published *Dead Souls* (1842), a satirisation of serfdom, seen by many critics as the first 'modern' Russian novel and his greatest longer work.

Gogol spent time living abroad in later life, settling in Rome and developing a passion for opera. As he got older, criticism of his work began to drain him, and he turned to religion, making a pilgrimage to Jerusalem in 1848. Upon his return to Russia, under the encouragement of the fanatical priest, Father Konstantinovskii, Gogol subjected himself to a fatal course of fasting. He died in Moscow in 1852, aged 42. He is seen by many contemporary critics as one of the greatest short story writers who has ever lived, and the Father of Russia's Golden Age of Realism.

CHAPTER I

IVAN IVANOVITCH AND IVAN NIKIFOROVITCH

A fine pelisse has Ivan Ivanovitch! splendid! And what lambskin! deuce take it, what lambskin! blue-black with silver lights. I'll forfeit, I know not what, if you find any one else owning such a one. Look at it, for heaven's sake, especially when he stands talking with any one! look at him side-ways: what a pleasure it is! To describe it is impossible: velvet! silver! fire! Nikolai the Wonder-worker, saint of God! why have I not such a pelisse? He had it made before Agafya Fedosyevna went to Kief. You know Agafya Fedosyevna who bit the assessor's ear off?

Ivan Ivanovitch is a very handsome man. What a house he has in Mirgorod! Around it on every side is a balcony on oaken pillars, and on the balcony are benches. Ivan Ivanovitch, when the weather gets too warm, throws off his pelisse and his remaining upper garments, and sits, in his shirt sleeves, on the balcony to observe what is going on in the courtyard and the street. What apples and pears he has under his very windows! You have but to open the window and the branches force themselves through into the room. All this is in front of the house; but you should see what he has in the garden. What is there not there? Plums, cherries, every sort of vegetable, sunflowers, cucumbers, melons, peas, a threshing-floor, and even a forge.

A very fine man, Ivan Ivanovitch! He is very fond of melons: they are his favourite food. As soon as he has dined, and come out on his balcony, in his shirt sleeves, he orders Gapka to bring two melons, and immediately cuts them himself, collects the seeds in a paper, and begins to eat. Then he orders Gapka to fetch the ink-bottle, and, with his own hand, writes this inscription on the paper of seeds: "These melons were eaten on such and such a date." If there was a guest present, then it reads, "Such and such a person assisted."

The late judge of Mirgorod always gazed at Ivan Ivanovitch's house with pleasure. The little house is very pretty. It pleases me because sheds and other little additions are built on to it on all sides; so that, looking at it from a distance, only roofs are visible, rising one above another, and greatly resembling a plate full of pancakes, or, better still, fungi growing on the trunk of a tree. Moreover, the roof is all overgrown with weeds: a willow, an oak, and two apple-trees lean their spreading branches against it. Through the trees peep little windows with carved and white-washed shutters, which project even into the street.

A very fine man, Ivan Ivanovitch! The commissioner of Poltava knows him too. Dorosh Tarasovitch Pukhivotchka, when he leaves Khorola, always goes to his house. And when Father Peter, the Protopope who lives at Koliberdas, invites a few guests, he always says that he knows of no one who so well fulfils all his Christian duties and understands so well how to live as Ivan Ivanovitch.

How time flies! More than ten years have already passed since he became a widower. He never had any children. Gapka has children and they run about the court-yard. Ivan Ivanovitch always gives each of them a cake, or a slice of melon, or a pear.

Gapka carries the keys of the storerooms and cellars; but the key of the large chest which stands in his bedroom, and that of the centre storeroom, Ivan Ivanovitch keeps himself; Gapka is a healthy girl, with ruddy cheeks and calves, and goes about in coarse cloth garments.

And what a pious man is Ivan Ivanovitch! Every Sunday he dons his pelisse and goes to church. On entering, he bows on all sides, generally stations himself in the choir, and sings a very good bass. When the service is over, Ivan Ivanovitch cannot refrain from passing the poor people in review. He probably would not have cared to undertake this tiresome work if his natural goodness had not urged him to it. "Goodday, beggar!" he generally said, selecting the most crippled old woman, in the most patched and threadbare garments. "Whence come you, my poor woman?"

"I come from the farm, sir. 'Tis two days since I have eaten or drunk: my own children drove me out."

"Poor soul! why did you come hither?"

"To beg alms, sir, to see whether some one will not give me at least enough for bread."

"Hm! so you want bread?" Ivan Ivanovitch generally inquired.

"How should it be otherwise? I am as hungry as a dog."

"Hm!" replied Ivan Ivanovitch usually, "and perhaps you would like butter too?"

"Yes; everything which your kindness will give; I will be content with all."

"Hm! Is butter better than bread?"

"How is a hungry person to choose? Anything you please, all is good." Thereupon the old woman generally extended her hand.

"Well, go with God's blessing," said Ivan Ivanovitch. "Why do you stand there? I'm not beating you." And turning to a second and a third with the same questions, he finally returns home, or goes to drink a little glass of vodka with his neighbour, Ivan Nikiforovitch, or the judge, or the chief of police.

Ivan Ivanovitch is very fond of receiving presents. They please him greatly.

A very fine man too is Ivan Nikiforovitch. They are such friends as the world never saw. Anton Prokofievitch Pupopuz, who goes about to this hour in his cinnamon-coloured surtout with blue sleeves and dines every Sunday with the judge, was in the habit of saying that the Devil himself had bound Ivan Ivanovitch and Ivan Nikiforovitch together with a rope: where one went, the other followed.

Ivan Nikiforovitch has never married. Although it was reported that he was married it was completely false. I know Ivan Nikiforovitch very well, and am able to state that he never even had any intention of marrying. Where do all these scandals originate? In the same way it was rumoured that Ivan Nikiforovitch was born with a tail! But this invention is so clumsy and at the same time so horrible and indecent that I do not even consider it necessary to refute it for the benefit of civilised readers, to whom it is doubtless known that only witches, and very few even of these, have tails. Witches, moreover, belong more to the feminine than to the masculine gender.

In spite of their great friendship, these rare friends are not always agreed between themselves. Their characters can best be judged by comparing them. Ivan Ivanovitch has the usual gift of speaking in an extremely pleasant manner. Heavens! How he does speak! The feeling can best be described by comparing it to that which you experience when some one combs your head or draws his finger softly across your heel. You listen and listen until you drop your head. Pleasant, exceedingly pleasant! like the sleep after a bath. Ivan Nikiforovitch, on the contrary, is more reticent; but if he once takes up his parable, look out for yourself! He can talk your head off.

Ivan Ivanovitch is tall and thin: Ivan Nikiforovitch is rather shorter in stature, but he makes it up in thickness. Ivan Ivanovitch's head is like a radish, tail down; Ivan Nikiforovitch's like a radish with the tail up. Ivan Ivanovitch lolls on the balcony in his shirt sleeves after dinner only: in the evening he dons his pelisse and goes out somewhere, either to the village shop, where he supplies flour, or into the fields to catch quail. Ivan Nikiforovitch lies all day at his porch: if the day is not too hot he generally turns his back to the sun and will not go anywhere. If it happens to occur to him in the morning he walks through the yard, inspects the domestic affairs, and retires again to his room. In early days he used to call on Ivan Ivanovitch. Ivan Ivanovitch is a very refined man, and never utters an impolite word. Ivan Nikiforovitch is not always on his guard. On such occasions Ivan Ivanovitch usually rises from his seat, and says, "Enough, enough, Ivan Nikiforovitch! It's better to go out at once than to utter such godless words."

Ivan Ivanovitch gets into a terrible rage if a fly falls into his beet-soup. Then he is fairly beside himself; he flings away his plate and the housekeeper catches it. Ivan Nikiforovitch is very fond of bathing; and when he gets up to the neck in water, orders a table and a samovar, or tea urn, to be placed on the water, for he is very fond of drinking tea in that cool position. Ivan Ivanovitch shaves twice a week; Ivan Nikiforovitch once. Ivan Ivanovitch is extremely curious. God preserve you if you begin to tell him anything and do not finish it! If he is displeased with anything he lets it be seen at once. It is very hard to tell from Ivan Nikiforovitch's countenance whether he is pleased or angry; even if he is rejoiced at anything, he will not show it. Ivan Ivanovitch is of a rather timid character: Ivan Nikiforovitch, on the contrary, has, as the saying is, such full folds in his trousers that if you were to inflate them you might put the courtyard, with its storehouses and buildings, inside them.

Ivan Ivanovitch has large, expressive eyes, of a snuff colour, and a mouth shaped something like the letter V; Ivan Nikiforovitch has small, yellowish eyes, quite concealed between heavy brows and fat cheeks; and his nose is the shape of a ripe plum. If Ivanovitch treats you to snuff, he always licks the cover of his box first with his tongue, then taps on it with his finger and says, as he raises it, if you are an acquaintance, "Dare I beg you, sir, to give me the pleasure?" if a stranger, "Dare I beg you, sir, though I have not the honour of knowing your rank, name, and family, to do me the favour?" but Ivan Nikiforovitch puts his box straight into your hand and merely adds, "Do me the favour." Neither Ivan

Ivanovitch nor Ivan Nikiforovitch loves fleas; and therefore, neither Ivan Ivanovitch nor Ivan Nikiforovitch will, on no account, admit a Jew with his wares, without purchasing of him remedies against these insects, after having first rated him well for belonging to the Hebrew faith.

But in spite of numerous dissimilarities, Ivan Ivanovitch and Ivan Nikiforovitch are both very fine fellows.

CHAPTER II

FROM WHICH MAY BE SEEN WHENCE AROSE THE DISCUSSION BETWEEN IVAN IVANOVITCH AND IVAN NIKIFOROVITCH

One morning—it was in July—Ivan Ivanovitch was lying on his balcony. The day was warm; the air was dry, and came in gusts. Ivan Ivanovitch had been to town, to the mower's, and at the farm, and had succeeded in asking all the muzhiks and women whom he met all manner of questions. He was fearfully tired and had laid down to rest. As he lay there, he looked at the storehouse, the courtyard, the sheds, the chickens running about, and thought to himself, "Heavens! What a well-to-do man I am! What is there that I have not? Birds, buildings, granaries, everything I take a fancy to; genuine distilled vodka; pears and plums in the orchard; poppies, cabbages, peas in the garden; what is there that I have not? I should like to know what there is that I have not?"

As he put this question to himself, Ivan Ivanovitch reflected; and meantime his eyes, in their search after fresh objects, crossed the fence into Ivan Nikiforovitch's yard and involuntarily took note of a curious sight. A fat woman was bringing out clothes, which had been packed away, and spreading them out on the line to air. Presently an old uniform with worn trimmings was swinging its sleeves in the air and embracing a brocade gown; from behind it peeped a court-coat, with buttons stamped with coats-of-arms, and moth-eaten collar; and white kersymere pantaloons with spots, which had once upon a time clothed Ivan Nikiforovitch's legs, and might now possibly fit his fingers. Behind them were speedily hung some more in the shape of the letter pi. Then came a blue Cossack jacket, which Ivan Nikiforovitch had had made twenty years before, when he was preparing to enter the militia, and allowed his moustache to grow. And one after another appeared a sword, projecting into the air like a spit, and the skirts of a grass-green caftan-like garment, with copper buttons the size of a five-kopek piece, unfolded themselves. From among the folds peeped a vest bound with gold, with a wide opening in front. The vest was soon concealed by an old petticoat belonging to his dead grandmother, with pockets which would have held a water-melon.

All these things piled together formed a very interesting spectacle for Ivan Ivanovitch; while the sun's rays, falling upon a blue or green sleeve, a red binding, or a scrap of gold brocade, or playing in the point of a sword, formed an unusual sight, similar to the representations of the Nativity given at farmhouses by wandering bands; particularly that part where the throng of people, pressing close together, gaze at King Herod in his golden crown or at Anthony leading his goat.

Presently the old woman crawled, grunting, from the storeroom, dragging after her an old-fashioned saddle with broken stirrups, worn leather holsters, and saddle-cloth, once red, with gilt embroidery and copper disks.

"Here's a stupid woman," thought Ivan Ivanovitch. "She'll be dragging Ivan Nikiforovitch out and airing him next."

Ivan Ivanovitch was not so far wrong in his surmise. Five minutes later, Ivan Nikiforovitch's nankeen trousers appeared, and took nearly half the yard to themselves. After that she fetched out a hat and a gun. "What's the meaning of this?" thought Ivan Ivanovitch. "I never knew Ivan Nikiforovitch had a gun. What does he want with it? Whether he shoots, or not, he keeps a gun! Of what use is it to him? But it's a splendid thing. I have long wanted just such a one. I should like that gun very much: I like to amuse myself with a gun. Hello, there, woman, woman!" shouted Ivan Ivanovitch, beckoning to her.

The old woman approached the fence.

"What's that you have there, my good woman?"

"A gun, as you see."

"What sort of a gun?"

"Who knows what sort of a gun? If it were mine, perhaps I should know what it is made of; but it is my master's, therefore I know nothing of it."

Ivan Ivanovitch rose, and began to examine the gun on all sides, and forgot to reprove the old woman for hanging it and the sword out to air.

"It must be iron," went on the old woman.

"Hm, iron! why iron?" said Ivan Ivanovitch. "Has your master had it long?"

"Yes; long, perhaps."

"It's a nice gun!" continued Ivan Ivanovitch. "I will ask him for it. What can he want with it? I'll make an exchange with him for it. Is your master at home, my good woman?"

"Yes."

"What is he doing? lying down?"

"Yes, lying down."

"Very well, I will come to him."

Ivan Ivanovitch dressed himself, took his well-seasoned stick for the benefit of the dogs, for, in Mirgorod, there are more dogs than people to be met in the street, and went out.

Although Ivan Nikiforovitch's house was next door to Ivan Ivanovitch's, so that you could have got from one to the other by climbing the fence, yet Ivan Ivanovitch went by way of the street. From the street it was necessary to turn into an alley which was so narrow that if two one-horse carts chanced to meet they could not get out, and were forced to remain there until the drivers, seizing the hind-wheels, dragged them back in opposite directions into the street, whilst pedestrians drew aside like flowers growing by the fence on either hand. Ivan Ivanovitch's waggon-shed adjoined this alley on one side; and on the other were Ivan Nikiforovitch's granary, gate, and pigeon-house.

Ivan Ivanovitch went up to the gate and rattled the latch. Within arose the barking of dogs; but the motley-haired pack ran back, wagging their tails when they saw the well-known face. Ivan Ivanovitch traversed the courtyard, in which were collected Indian doves, fed by Ivan Nikiforovitch's own hand, melon-rinds, vegetables, broken wheels, barrel-hoops, and a small boy wallowing with dirty blouse—a picture such as painters love. The shadows of the fluttering clothes covered nearly the whole of the yard and lent it a degree of coolness. The woman greeted him with a bend of her head and stood, gaping, in one spot. The front of the house was adorned with a small porch, with its roof supported on two oak pillars—a welcome protection from the sun, which at that season in Little Russia loves not to jest, and bathes the pedestrian from head to foot in perspiration. It may be judged how powerful Ivan Ivanovitch's desire to obtain the coveted article was when he made up his mind, at such an hour, to depart from his usual custom, which was to walk abroad only in the evening.

The room which Ivan Ivanovitch entered was quite dark, for the shutters were closed; and the ray of sunlight passing through a hole made in one of them took on the colours of the rainbow, and, striking the opposite wall, sketched upon it a parti-coloured picture of the outlines of roofs, trees, and the clothes suspended in the yard, only upside down. This gave the room a peculiar half-light.

"God assist you!" said Ivan Ivanovitch.

"Ah! how do you do, Ivan Ivanovitch?" replied a voice from the corner of the room. Then only did Ivan Ivanovitch perceive Ivan Nikiforovitch lying upon a rug which was spread on the floor. "Excuse me for appearing before you in a state of nature."

"Not at all. You have been asleep, Ivan Nikiforovitch?"

"I have been asleep. Have you been asleep, Ivan Ivanovitch?"

"I have."

"And now you have risen?"

"Now I have risen. Christ be with you, Ivan Nikiforovitch! How can you sleep until this time? I have just come from the farm. There's very fine barley on the road, charming! and the hay is tall and soft and golden!"

"Gorpina!" shouted Ivan Nikiforovitch, "fetch Ivan Ivanovitch some vodka, and some pastry and sour cream!"

"Fine weather we're having to-day."

"Don't praise it, Ivan Ivanovitch! Devil take it! You can't get away from the heat."

"Now, why need you mention the devil! Ah, Ivan Nikiforovitch! you will recall my words when it's too late. You will suffer in the next world for such godless words."

"How have I offended you, Ivan Ivanovitch? I have not attacked your father nor your mother. I don't know how I have insulted you."

"Enough, enough, Ivan Nikiforovitch!"

"By Heavens, Ivan Ivanovitch, I did not insult you!"

"It's strange that the quails haven't come yet to the whistle."

"Think what you please, but I have not insulted you in any way."

"I don't know why they don't come," said Ivan Ivanovitch, as if he did not hear Ivan Nikiforovitch; "it is more than time for them already; but they seem to need more time for some reason."

"You say that the barley is good?"

"Splendid barley, splendid!"

A silence ensued.

"So you are having your clothes aired, Ivan Nikiforovitch?" said Ivan Ivanovitch at length.

"Yes; those cursed women have ruined some beautiful clothes; almost new they were too. Now I'm having them aired; the cloth is fine and good. They only need turning to make them fit to wear again."

"One thing among them pleased me extremely, Ivan Nikiforovitch."

"What was that?"

"Tell me, please, what use do you make of the gun that has been put to air with the clothes?" Here Ivan Ivanovitch offered his snuff. "May I ask you to do me the favour?"

"By no means! take it yourself; I will use my own." Thereupon Ivan Nikiforovitch felt about him, and got hold of his snuff-box. "That stupid woman! So she hung the gun out to air. That Jew at Sorotchintzi makes good snuff. I don't know what he puts in it, but it is so very fragrant. It is a little like tansy. Here, take a little and chew it; isn't it like tansy?"

"Ivan Nikiforovitch, I want to talk about that gun; what are you going to do with it? You don't need it."

"Why don't I need it? I might want to go shooting."

"God be with you, Ivan Nikiforovitch! When will you go shooting? At the millennium, perhaps? So far as I know, or any one can recollect, you never killed even a duck; yes, and you are not built to go shooting. You have a dignified bearing and figure; how are you to drag yourself about the marshes, especially when your garment, which it is not polite to mention in conversation by name, is being aired at this very moment? No; you require rest, repose." Ivan Ivanovitch as has been hinted at above, employed uncommonly

18

picturesque language when it was necessary to persuade any one. How he talked! Heavens, how he could talk! "Yes, and you require polite actions. See here, give it to me!"

"The idea! The gun is valuable; you can't find such guns anywhere nowadays. I bought it of a Turk when I joined the militia; and now, to give it away all of a sudden! Impossible! It is an indispensable article."

"Indispensable for what?"

"For what? What if robbers should attack the house?... Indispensable indeed! Glory to God! I know that a gun stands in my storehouse."

"A fine gun that! Why, Ivan Nikiforovitch, the lock is ruined."

"What do you mean by ruined? It can be set right; all that needs to be done is to rub it with hemp-oil, so that it may not rust."

"I see in your words, Ivan Nikiforovitch, anything but a friendly disposition towards me. You will do nothing for me in token of friendship."

"How can you say, Ivan Ivanovitch, that I show you no friendship? You ought to be ashamed of yourself. Your oxen pasture on my steppes and I have never interfered with them. When you go to Poltava, you always ask for my waggon, and what then? Have I ever refused? Your children climb over the fence into my yard and play with my dogs—I never say anything; let them play, so long as they touch nothing; let them play!"

"If you won't give it to me, then let us make some exchange."

"What will you give me for it?" Thereupon Ivan Nikiforovitch raised himself on his elbow, and looked at Ivan Ivanovitch.

"I will give you my dark-brown sow, the one I have fed in the sty. A magnificent sow. You'll see, she'll bring you a litter of pigs next year."

"I do not see, Ivan Ivanovitch, how you can talk so. What could I do with your sow? Make a funeral dinner for the devil?"

"Again! You can't get along without the devil! It's a sin! by Heaven, it's a sin, Ivan Nikiforovitch!"

"What do you mean, Ivan Ivanovitch, by offering the deuce knows what kind of a sow for my gun?"

"Why is she 'the deuce knows what,' Ivan Nikiforovitch?"

"Why? You can judge for yourself perfectly well; here's the gun, a known thing; but the deuce knows what that sow is like! If it had not been you who said it, Ivan Ivanovitch, I might have put an insulting construction on it."

"What defect have you observed in the sow?"

"For what do you take me—for a sow?"

"Sit down, sit down! I won't—No matter about your gun; let it rot and rust where it stands in the corner of the storeroom. I don't want to say anything more about it!"

After this a pause ensued.

"They say," began Ivan Ivanovitch, "that three kings have declared war against our Tzar."

"Yes, Peter Feodorovitch told me so. What sort of war is this, and why is it?"

"I cannot say exactly, Ivan Nikiforovitch, what the cause is. I suppose the kings want us to adopt the Turkish faith."

"Fools! They would have it," said Ivan Nikiforovitch, raising his head.

"So, you see, our Tzar has declared war on them in consequence. 'No,' says he, 'do you adopt the faith of Christ!'"

"Oh, our people will beat them, Ivan Ivanovitch!"

"They will. So you won't exchange the gun, Ivan Nikiforovitch?"

"It's a strange thing to me, Ivan Ivanovitch, that you, who seem to be a man distinguished for sense, should talk such nonsense. What a fool I should be!"

"Sit down, sit down. God be with it! let it burst! I won't mention it again."

At this moment lunch was brought in.

Ivan Ivanovitch drank a glass and ate a pie with sour cream. "Listen, Ivan Nikiforovitch: I will give you, besides the sow, two sacks of oats. You did not sow any oats. You'll have to buy some this year in any case."

"By Heaven, Ivan Ivanovitch, I must tell you you are very foolish! Who ever heard of swapping a gun for two sacks of oats? Never fear, you don't offer your coat."

"But you forget, Ivan Nikiforovitch, that I am to give you the sow too."

"What! two sacks of oats and a sow for a gun?"

"Why, is it too little?"

"For a gun?"

"Of course, for a gun."

"Two sacks for a gun?"

"Two sacks, not empty, but filled with oats; and you've forgotten the sow."

"Kiss your sow; and if you don't like that, then go to the Evil One!"

"Oh, get angry now, do! See here; they'll stick your tongue full of red-hot needles in the other world for such godless words. After a conversation with you, one has to wash one's face and hands and fumigate one's self."

"Excuse me, Ivan Ivanovitch; my gun is a choice thing, a most curious thing; and besides, it is a very agreeable decoration in a room."

"You go on like a fool about that gun of yours, Ivan Nikiforovitch," said Ivan Ivanovitch with vexation; for he was beginning to be really angry.

"And you, Ivan Ivanovitch, are a regular goose!"

If Ivan Nikiforovitch had not uttered that word they would not have quarrelled, but would have parted friends as usual; but now things took quite another turn. Ivan Ivanovitch flew into a rage.

"What was that you said, Ivan Nikiforovitch?" he said, raising his voice.

"I said you were like a goose, Ivan Ivanovitch!"

"How dare you, sir, forgetful of decency and the respect due to a man's rank and family, insult him with such a disgraceful name!"

"What is there disgraceful about it? And why are you flourishing your hands so, Ivan Ivanovitch?"

"How dared you, I repeat, in disregard of all decency, call me a goose?"

"I spit on your head, Ivan Ivanovitch! What are you screeching about?"

Ivan Ivanovitch could no longer control himself. His lips quivered; his mouth lost its usual V shape, and became like the letter O; he glared so that he was terrible to look at. This very rarely happened with Ivan Ivanovitch: it was necessary that he should be extremely angry at first.

"Then, I declare to you," exclaimed Ivan Ivanovitch, "that I will no longer know you!"

"A great pity! By Heaven, I shall never weep on that account!" retorted Ivan Nikiforovitch. He lied, by Heaven, he lied! for it was very annoying to him.

"I will never put my foot inside your house gain!"

"Oho, ho!" said Ivan Nikiforovitch, vexed, yet not knowing himself what to do, and rising to his feet, contrary to his custom. "Hey, there, woman, boy!" Thereupon there appeared at the door the same fat woman and the small boy, now enveloped in a long and wide coat. "Take Ivan Ivanovitch by the arms and lead him to the door!"

"What! a nobleman?" shouted Ivan Ivanovitch with a feeling of vexation and dignity. "Just do it if you dare! Come on! I'll annihilate you and your stupid master. The crows won't be able to find your bones." Ivan Ivanovitch spoke with uncommon force when his spirit was up.

The group presented a striking picture: Ivan Nikiforovitch standing in the middle of the room; the woman with her mouth wide open and a senseless, terrified look on her face, and Ivan Ivanovitch with uplifted hand, as the Roman tribunes are depicted. This was a magnificent spectacle: and yet there was but one spectator; the boy in the ample coat, who stood quite quietly and picked his nose with his finger.

Finally Ivan Ivanovitch took his hat. "You have behaved well, Ivan Nikiforovitch, extremely well! I shall remember it."

"Go, Ivan Ivanovitch, go! and see that you don't come in my way: if you do, I'll beat your ugly face to a jelly, Ivan Ivanovitch!"

"Take that, Ivan Nikiforovitch!" retorted Ivan Ivanovitch, making an insulting gesture and banged the door, which squeaked and flew open again behind him.

Ivan Nikiforovitch appeared at it and wanted to add something more; but Ivan Ivanovitch did not glance back and hastened from the yard.

CHAPTER III

WHAT TOOK PLACE AFTER IVAN IVANOVITCH'S QUARREL WITH IVAN NIKIFOROVITCH

And thus two respectable men, the pride and honour of Mirgorod, had quarrelled, and about what? About a bit of nonsense—a goose. They would not see each other, broke off all connection, though hitherto they had been known as the most inseparable friends. Every day Ivan Ivanovitch and Ivan Nikiforovitch had sent to inquire about each other's health, and often conversed together from their balconies and said such charming things as did the heart good to listen to. On Sundays, Ivan Ivanovitch, in his lambskin pelisse, and Ivan Nikiforovitch, in his cinnamon-coloured nankeen spencer, used to set out for church almost arm in arm; and if Ivan Ivanovitch, who had remarkably sharp eyes, was the first to catch sight of a puddle or any dirt in the street, which sometimes happened in Mirgorod, he always said to Ivan Nikiforovitch, "Look out! don't put your foot there, it's dirty." Ivan Nikiforovitch, on his side, exhibited the same touching tokens of friendship; and whenever he chanced to be standing, always held out his hand to Ivan Ivanovitch with his snuff-box, saying: "Do me the favour!" And what fine managers both were!—And these two friends!—When I heard of it, it struck me like a flash of lightning. For a long time I would not believe it. Ivan Ivanovitch quarrelling with Ivan Nikiforovitch! Such worthy people! What is to be depended upon, then, in this world?

When Ivan Ivanovitch reached home, he remained for some time in a state of strong excitement. He usually went, first of all, to the stable to see whether his mare was eating her hay; for he had a bay mare with a white star on her forehead, and a very pretty little mare she was too; then to feed the turkeys and the little pigs with his own hand, and then to his room, where he either made wooden dishes, for he could make various vessels of wood very tastefully, quite as well as any turner, or read a book printed by Liubia, Garia, and Popoff (Ivan Ivanovitch could never remember the name, because the serving-maid had long before torn off the top part of the title-page while amusing the children), or rested on the balcony. But now he did not betake himself to any of his ordinary occupations. Instead, on encountering Gapka, he at once began to scold her for loitering about without any occupation, though she was carrying groats to the kitchen; flung a stick at a cock which came upon the balcony for his customary treat; and when the dirty little boy, in his little torn blouse, ran up to him and shouted: "Papa, papa! give me a honey-cake," he threatened him and stamped at him so fiercely that the frightened child fled, God knows whither.

But at last he bethought himself, and began to busy himself about his every-day duties. He dined late, and it was almost night when he lay down to rest on the balcony. A good beet-soup with pigeons, which Gapka had cooked for him, quite drove from his mind the occurrences of the morning. Again Ivan Ivanovitch began to gaze at his belongings with satisfaction. At length his eye rested on the neighbouring yard; and he said to himself, "I have not been to Ivan Nikiforovitch's to-day: I'll go there now." So saying, Ivan Ivanovitch took his stick and his hat, and directed his steps to the street; but scarcely had he passed through the gate than he recollected the quarrel, spit, and turned back. Almost the same thing happened at Ivan Nikiforovitch's house. Ivan Ivanovitch saw the woman put her foot on the fence, with the intention of climbing over into his yard, when suddenly Ivan Nikiforovitch's voice was heard crying: "Come back! it won't do!" But Ivan Ivanovitch found it very tiresome. It is quite possible that these worthy men would have made their peace next day if a certain occurrence in Ivan Nikiforovitch's house had not destroyed all hopes and poured oil upon the fire of enmity which was ready to die out.

On the evening of that very day, Agafya Fedosyevna arrived at Ivan Nikiforovitch's. Agafya Fedosyevna was not Ivan Nikiforovitch's relative, nor his sister-in-law, nor even his fellow-godparent. There seemed to be no reason why she should come to him, and he was not particularly glad of her company; still, she came, and lived on him for weeks at a time, and even longer. Then she took possession of the keys and took the management of the whole house into her own hands. This was extremely displeasing to Ivan Nikiforovitch; but he, to his amazement, obeyed her like a child; and although he occasionally attempted to dispute, yet Agafya Fedosyevna always got the better of him.

I must confess that I do not understand why things are so arranged, that women should seize us by the nose as deftly as they do the handle of a teapot. Either their hands are so constructed or else our noses are good for nothing else. And notwithstanding the fact that Ivan Nikiforovitch's nose somewhat resembled a plum, she grasped that nose and led him about after her like a dog. He even, in her presence, involuntarily altered his ordinary manner of life.

Agafya Fedosyevna wore a cap on her head, and a coffee-coloured cloak with yellow flowers and had three warts on her nose. Her figure was like a cask, and it would have been as hard to tell where to look for her waist as for her to see her nose without a mirror. Her feet were small and shaped like two cushions. She talked scandal, ate boiled beet-soup in the morning, and swore extremely; and amidst all these various occupations her countenance never for one instant changed its expression, which phenomenon, as a rule, women alone are capable of displaying.

As soon as she arrived, everything went wrong.

"Ivan Nikiforovitch, don't you make peace with him, nor ask his forgiveness; he wants to ruin you; that's the kind of man he is! you don't know him yet!" That cursed woman whispered and whispered, and managed so that Ivan Nikiforovitch would not even hear Ivan Ivanovitch mentioned.

Everything assumed another aspect. If his neighbour's dog ran into the yard, it was beaten within an inch of its life; the children, who climbed over the fence, were sent back with howls, their little shirts stripped up, and marks of a switch behind. Even the old woman, when Ivan Ivanovitch ventured to ask her about something, did something so insulting that Ivan Ivanovitch, being an extremely delicate man, only spit, and muttered, "What a nasty woman! even worse than her master!"

Finally, as a climax to all the insults, his hated neighbour built a goose-shed right against his fence at the spot where they usually climbed over, as if with the express intention of redoubling the insult. This shed, so hateful to Ivan Ivanovitch, was constructed with diabolical swiftness—in one day.

This aroused wrath and a desire for revenge in Ivan Ivanovitch. He showed no signs of bitterness, in spite of the fact that the shed encroached on his land; but his heart beat so violently that it was extremely difficult for him to preserve his calm appearance.

He passed the day in this manner. Night came—Oh, if I were a painter, how magnificently I would depict the night's charms! I would describe how all Mirgorod sleeps; how steadily the myriads of stars gaze down upon it; how the apparent quiet is filled far and near with the barking of dogs; how the love-sick sacristan steals past them, and scales the fence with knightly fearlessness; how the white walls of the houses, bathed in the moonlight, grow whiter still, the overhanging trees darker; how the shadows of the trees fall blacker, the flowers and the silent grass become more fragrant, and the crickets, unharmonious cavaliers of the night, strike up their rattling song in friendly fashion on all sides. I would describe how, in one of the little, low-roofed, clay houses, the black-browed village maid, tossing on her lonely couch, dreams with heaving bosom of some hussar's spurs and moustache, and how the moonlight smiles upon her cheeks. I would describe how the black shadows of the bats flit along the white road before they alight upon the white chimneys of the cottages.

But it would hardly be within my power to depict Ivan Ivanovitch as he crept out that night, saw in hand; or the various emotions written on his countenance! Quietly, most quietly, he crawled along and climbed upon the goose-shed. Ivan Nikiforovitch's dogs knew nothing, as yet, of the quarrel between them; and so they permitted him, as an old friend, to enter the shed, which rested upon four oaken posts. Creeping up to the nearest post he applied his saw and began to cut. The noise produced by the saw caused him to glance about him every moment, but the recollection of the insult restored his courage. The first post was sawed through. Ivan Ivanovitch began upon the next. His eyes burned and he saw nothing for terror.

All at once he uttered an exclamation and became petrified with fear. A ghost appeared to him; but he speedily recovered himself on perceiving that it was a goose, thrusting its neck out at him. Ivan Ivanovitch spit with vexation and proceeded with his work. The second post was sawed through; the building trembled. His heart beat so violently when he began on the third, that he had to stop several times. The post was more than half sawed through when the frail building quivered violently.

Ivan Ivanovitch had barely time to spring back when it came down with a crash. Seizing his saw, he ran home in the greatest terror and flung himself upon his bed, without having sufficient courage to peep from the window at the consequences of his terrible deed. It seemed to him as though Ivan Nikiforovitch's entire household—the old woman, Ivan Nikiforovitch, the boy in the endless coat, all with sticks, and led by Agafya Fedosyevna—were coming to tear down and destroy his house.

Ivan Ivanovitch passed the whole of the following day in a perfect fever. It seemed to him that his detested neighbour would set fire to his house at least in revenge for this; and so he gave orders to Gapka to keep a constant lookout, everywhere, and see whether dry straw were laid against it anywhere. Finally, in order to forestall Ivan Nikiforovitch, he determined to enter a complaint against him before the district judge of Mirgorod. In what it consisted can be learned from the following chapter.

CHAPTER IV

WHAT TOOK PLACE BEFORE THE DISTRICT JUDGE OF MIRGOROD

A wonderful town is Mirgorod! How many buildings are there with straw, rush, and even wooden roofs! On the right is a street, on the left a street, and fine fences everywhere. Over them twine hop-vines, upon them hang pots; from behind them the sunflowers show their sun-like heads, poppies blush, fat pumpkins peep; all is luxury itself! The fence is invariably garnished with articles which render it still more picturesque: woman's widespread undergarments of checked woollen stuff, shirts, or trousers. There is no such thing as theft or rascality in Mirgorod, so everybody hangs upon his fence whatever strikes his fancy. If you go on to the square, you will surely stop and admire the view: such a wonderful pool is there! The finest you ever saw. It occupies nearly the whole of the square. A truly magnificent pool! The houses and cottages, which at a distance might be mistaken for hayricks, stand around it, lost in admiration of its beauty.

But I agree with those who think that there is no better house than that of the district judge. Whether it is of oak or birch is nothing to the point; but it has, my dear sirs, eight windows! eight windows in a row, looking directly on the square and upon that watery expanse which I have just mentioned, and which the chief of police calls a lake. It alone is painted the colour of granite. All the other houses in Mirgorod are merely whitewashed. Its roof is of wood, and would have been even painted red, had not the government clerks eaten the oil which had been prepared for that purpose, as it happened during a fast; and so the roof remained unpainted. Towards the square projects a porch, which the chickens frequently visit, because that porch is nearly always strewn with grain or something edible, not intentionally, but through the carelessness of visitors.

The house is divided into two parts: one of which is the court-room; the other the jail. In the half which contains the court-room are two neat, whitewashed rooms, the front one for clients, the other having a table adorned with ink-spots, and with a looking-glass upon it, and four oak chairs with tall backs; whilst along the wall stand iron-bound chests, in which are preserved bundles of papers relating to district law-suits. Upon one of the chests stood at that time a pair of boots, polished with wax.

The court had been open since morning. The judge, a rather stout man, though thinner than Ivan Nikiforovitch, with a good-natured face, a greasy dressing-gown, a pipe, and a cup of tea, was conversing with the clerk of the court.

The judge's lips were directly under his nose, so that he could snuff his upper lip as much as he liked. It served him instead of a snuff-box, for the snuff intended for his nose almost always lodged upon it. So the judge was talking with the assistant. A barefooted girl stood holding a tray with cups at once side of them. At the end of the table, the secretary was reading the decision in some case, but in such a mournful and monotonous voice that the condemned man himself would have fallen asleep while listening to it. The judge, no doubt, would have been the first to do so had he not entered into an engrossing conversation while it was going on.

"I expressly tried to find out," said the judge, sipping his already cold tea from the cup, "how they manage to sing so well. I had a splendid thrush two years ago. Well, all of a sudden he was completely done for, and began to sing, God knows what! He got worse and worse and worse and worse as time went on; he began to rattle and get hoarse—just good for nothing! And this is how it happened: a little lump, not so big as a pea, had come under his throat. It was only necessary to prick that little swelling with a needle—Zachar Prokofievitch taught me that; and, if you like, I'll just tell you how it was. I went to him—"

"Shall I read another, Demyan Demyanovitch?" broke in the secretary, who had not been reading for several minutes.

"Have you finished already? Only think how quickly! And I did not hear a word of it! Where is it? Give it me and I'll sign it. What else have you there?"

"The case of Cossack Bokitok for stealing a cow."

"Very good; read it!—Yes, so I went to him—I can even tell you in detail how he entertained me. There was vodka, and dried sturgeon, excellent! Yes, not our sturgeon," there the judge smacked his tongue and smiled, upon which his nose took a sniff at its usual snuff-box, "such as our Mirgorod shops sell us. I ate no herrings, for, as you know, they give me heart-burn; but I tasted the caviare—very fine caviare, too! There's no doubt it, excellent! Then I drank some peach-brandy, real gentian. There was saffron-brandy also; but, as you know, I never take that. You see, it was all very good. In the first place, to whet your appetite, as they say, and then to satisfy it—Ah! speak of an angel," exclaimed the judge, all at once, catching sight of Ivan Ivanovitch as he entered.

"God be with us! I wish you a good-morning," said Ivan Ivanovitch, bowing all round with his usual politeness. How well he understood the art of fascinating everybody in his manner! I never beheld such refinement. He knew his own worth quite well, and therefore looked for universal respect as his due. The judge himself handed Ivan Ivanovitch a chair; and his nose inhaled all the snuff resting on his upper lip, which, with him, was always a sign of great pleasure.

"What will you take, Ivan Ivanovitch?" he inquired: "will you have a cup of tea?"

"No, much obliged," replied Ivan Ivanovitch, as he bowed and seated himself.

"Do me the favour—one little cup," repeated the judge.

"No, thank you; much obliged for your hospitality," replied Ivan Ivanovitch, and rose, bowed, and sat down again.

"Just one little cup," repeated the judge.

"No, do not trouble yourself, Demyan Demyanovitch." Whereupon Ivan Ivanovitch again rose, bowed, and sat down.

"A little cup!"

"Very well, then, just a little cup," said Ivan Ivanovitch, and reached out his hand to the tray. Heavens! What a height of refinement there was in that man! It is impossible to describe what a pleasant impression such manners produce!

"Will you not have another cup?"

"I thank you sincerely," answered Ivan Ivanovitch, turning his cup upside down upon the tray and bowing.

"Do me the favour, Ivan Ivanovitch."

"I cannot; much obliged." Thereupon Ivan Ivanovitch bowed and sat down.

"Ivan Ivanovitch, for the sake of our friendship, just one little cup!"

"No: I am extremely indebted for your hospitality." So saying, Ivan Ivanovitch bowed and seated himself.

"Only a cup, one little cup!"

Ivan Ivanovitch put his hand out to the tray and took a cup. Oh, the deuce! How can a man contrive to support his dignity!

"Demyan Demyanovitch," said Ivan Ivanovitch, swallowing the last drain, "I have pressing business with you; I want to enter a complaint."

Then Ivan Ivanovitch set down his cup, and drew from his pocket a sheet of stamped paper, written over. "A complaint against my enemy, my declared enemy."

"And who is that?"

"Ivan Nikiforovitch Dovgotchkun."

At these words, the judge nearly fell off his chair. "What do you say?" he exclaimed, clasping his hands; "Ivan Ivanovitch, is this you?"

"You see yourself that it is I."

"The Lord and all the saints be with you! What! You! Ivan Ivanovitch! you have fallen out with Ivan Nikiforovitch! Is it your mouth which says that? Repeat it! Is not some one hid behind you who is speaking instead of you?"

"What is there incredible about it? I can't endure the sight of him: he has done me a deadly injury—he has insulted my honour."

"Holy Trinity! How am I to believe my mother now? Why, every day, when I quarrel with my sister, the old woman says, 'Children, you live together like dogs. If you would only take pattern by Ivan Ivanovitch and Ivan Nikiforovitch, they are friends indeed! such friends! such worthy people!' There you are with your friend! Tell me what this is about. How is it?"

"It is a delicate business, Demyan Demyanovitch; it is impossible to relate it in words: be pleased rather to read my plaint. Here, take it by this side; it is more convenient."

"Read it, Taras Tikhonovitch," said the judge, turning to the secretary.

Taras Tikhonovitch took the plaint; and blowing his nose, as all district judges' secretaries blow their noses, with the assistance of two fingers, he began to read:—

"From the nobleman and landed proprietor of the Mirgorod District, Ivan Pererepenko, son of Ivan, a plaint: concerning which the following points are to be noted:—

"1. Ivan Dovgotchkun, son of Nikifor, nobleman, known to all the world for his godless acts, which inspire disgust, and in lawlessness exceed all bounds, on the seventh day of July of this year 1810, inflicted upon me a deadly insult, touching my personal honour, and likewise tending to the humiliation and confusion of my rank and family. The said nobleman, of repulsive aspect, has also a pugnacious disposition, and is full to overflowing with blasphemy and quarrelsome words."

Here the reader paused for an instant to blow his nose again; but the judge folded his hands in approbation and murmured to himself, "What a ready pen! Lord! how this man does write!"

Ivan Ivanovitch requested that the reading might proceed, and Taras Tikhonovitch went on:—

"The said Ivan Dovgotchkun, son of Nikifor, when I went to him with a friendly proposition, called me publicly by an epithet insulting and injurious to my honour, namely, a goose, whereas it is known to the whole district of Mirgorod, that I never was named after that disgusting creature, and have no intention of ever being named after it. The proof of my noble extraction is that, in the baptismal register to be found in the Church of the Three Bishops, the day of my birth, and likewise the fact of my baptism, are inscribed. But a goose, as is well known to every one who has any knowledge of science, cannot be inscribed in the baptismal register; for a goose is not a man but a fowl; which, likewise, is sufficiently well known even to persons who have not been to college. But the said evil-minded nobleman, being privy to all these facts, affronted me with the aforesaid foul word, for no other purpose than to offer a deadly insult to my rank and station.

"2. And the same impolite and indecent nobleman, moreover, attempted injury to my property, inherited by me from my father, a member of the clerical profession, Ivan Pererepenko, son of Onisieff, of blessed memory, inasmuch that he, contrary to all law, transported directly opposite my porch a goose-shed, which was done with no other intention that to emphasise the insult offered me; for the said shed had, up to that time, stood in a very suitable situation, and was still sufficiently strong. But the loathsome intention of the aforesaid nobleman consisted simply in this: viz., in making me a witness of unpleasant occurrences; for it is well known that no man goes into a shed, much less into a goose-shed, for polite purposes. In the execution of his lawless deed, the two front posts trespassed on my land, received by me during the lifetime of my father, Ivan Pererepenko, son of Onisieff, of blessed memory, beginning at the granary, thence in a straight line to the spot where the women wash the pots.

"3. The above-described nobleman, whose very name and surname inspire thorough disgust, cherishes in his mind a malicious design to burn me in my own house. Which the infallible signs, hereinafter mentioned, fully demonstrate; in the first place, the said wicked nobleman has begun to emerge frequently from his apartments, which he never did formerly on account of his laziness and the disgusting corpulence of his body; in the second place, in his servants' apartments, adjoining the fence, surrounding my own land, received by me from my father of blessed memory, Ivan Pererepenko, son of Onisieff, a light burns every day, and for a remarkably long period of time, which is also a clear proof of the fact. For hitherto, owing to his repulsive niggardliness, not only the tallow-candle but also the grease-lamp has been extinguished.

"And therefore I pray that the said nobleman, Ivan Dovgotchkun, son of Nikifor, being plainly guilty of incendiarism, of insult to my rank, name, and family, and of illegal appropriation of my property, and, worse than all else, of malicious and deliberate addition to my surname, of the nickname of goose, be condemned by the court, to fine, satisfaction, costs, and damages, and, being chained, be removed to the town jail, and that judgment be rendered upon this, my plaint, immediately and without delay.

"Written and composed by Ivan Pererepenko, son of Ivan, nobleman, and landed proprietor of Mirgorod."

After the reading of the plaint was concluded, the judge approached Ivanovitch, took him by the button, and began to talk to him after this fashion: "What are you doing, Ivan Ivanovitch? Fear God! throw away that plaint, let it go! may Satan carry it off! Better take Ivan Nikiforovitch by the hand and kiss him, buy some Santurinski or Nikopolski liquor, make a punch, and call me in. We will drink it up together and forget all unpleasantness."

"No, Demyan Demyanovitch! it's not that sort of an affair," said Ivan Ivanovitch, with the dignity which always became him so well; "it is not an affair which can be arranged by a friendly agreement. Farewell! Good-day to you, too, gentlemen," he continued with the same dignity, turning to them all. "I hope that my plaint will lead to proper action being taken;" and out he went, leaving all present in a state of stupefaction.

The judge sat down without uttering a word; the secretary took a pinch of snuff; the clerks upset some broken fragments of bottles which served for inkstands; and the judge himself, in absence of mind, spread out a puddle of ink upon the table with his finger.

"What do you say to this, Dorofei Trofimovitch?" said the judge, turning to the assistant after a pause.

"I've nothing to say," replied the clerk.

"What things do happen!" continued the judge. He had not finished saying this before the door creaked and the front half of Ivan Nikiforovitch presented itself in the court-room; the rest of him remaining in the ante-room. The appearance of Ivan Nikiforovitch, and in court too, seemed so extraordinary that the judge screamed; the secretary stopped reading; one clerk, in his frieze imitation of a dress-coat, took his pen in his lips; and the other swallowed a fly. Even the constable on duty and the watchman, a discharged soldier who up to that moment had stood by the door scratching about his dirty tunic, with chevrons on its arm, dropped his jaw and trod on some one's foot.

"What chance brings you here? How is your health, Ivan Nikiforovitch?"

But Ivan Nikiforovitch was neither dead nor alive; for he was stuck fast in the door, and could not take a step either forwards or backwards. In vain did the judge shout into the ante-room that some one there should push Ivan Nikiforovitch forward into the court-room. In the ante-room there was only one old woman with a petition, who, in spite of all the efforts of her bony hands, could accomplish nothing. Then one of the clerks, with thick lips, a thick nose, eyes which looked askance and intoxicated, broad shoulders, and ragged elbows, approached the front half of Ivan Nikiforovitch, crossed his hands for him as though he had been a child, and winked at the old soldier, who braced his knee against Ivan Nikiforovitch's belly, so, in spite of the latter's piteous moans, he was squeezed out into the ante-room. Then they pulled the bolts, and opened the other half of the door. Meanwhile the clerk and his assistant, breathing hard with their friendly exertions, exhaled such a strong odour that the court-room seemed temporarily turned into a drinking-room.

"Are you hurt, Ivan Nikiforovitch? I will tell my mother to send you a decoction of brandy, with which you need but to rub your back and stomach and all your pains will disappear."

But Ivan Nikiforovitch dropped into a chair, and could utter no word beyond prolonged oh's. Finally, in a faint and barely audible voice from fatigue, he exclaimed, "Wouldn't you like some?" and drawing his snuff-box from his pocket, added, "Help yourself, if you please."

"Very glad to see you," replied the judge; "but I cannot conceive what made you put yourself to so much trouble, and favour us with so unexpected an honour."

"A plaint!" Ivan Nikiforovitch managed to ejaculate.

"A plaint? What plaint?"

"A complaint..." here his asthma entailed a prolonged pause—"Oh! a complaint against that rascal—Ivan Ivanovitch Pererepenko!"

"And you too! Such particular friends! A complaint against such a benevolent man?"

"He's Satan himself!" ejaculated Ivan Nikiforovitch abruptly.

The judge crossed himself.

"Take my plaint, and read it."

"There is nothing to be done. Read it, Taras Tikhonovitch," said the judge, turning to the secretary with an expression of displeasure, which caused his nose to sniff at his upper lip, which generally occurred only as a sign of great enjoyment. This independence on the part of his nose caused the judge still greater vexation. He pulled out his handkerchief, and rubbed off all the snuff from his upper lip in order to punish it for its daring.

The secretary, having gone through the usual performance, which he always indulged in before he began to read, that is to say, blowing his nose without the aid of a pocket-handkerchief, began in his ordinary voice, in the following manner:—

"Ivan Dovgotchkun, son of Nikifor, nobleman of the Mirgorod District, presents a plaint, and begs to call attention to the following points:—

"1. Through his hateful malice and plainly manifested ill-will, the person calling himself a nobleman, Ivan Pererepenko, son of Ivan, perpetrates against me every manner of injury, damage, and like spiteful deeds, which inspire me with terror. Yesterday afternoon, like a brigand and thief, with axes, saws, chisels, and various locksmith's tools, he came by night into my yard and into my own goose-shed located within it, and with his own hand, and in outrageous manner, destroyed it; for which very illegal and burglarious deed on my side I gave no manner of cause.

"2. The same nobleman Pererepenko has designs upon my life; and on the 7th of last month, cherishing this design in secret, he came to me, and began, in a friendly and insidious manner, to ask of me a gun which was in my chamber, and offered me for it, with the miserliness peculiar to him, many worthless objects, such as a brown sow and two sacks of oats. Divining at that time his criminal intentions, I endeavoured in every way to dissuade him from it: but the said rascal and scoundrel, Ivan Pererepenko, son of Ivan, abused me like a muzhik, and since that time has cherished against me an irreconcilable enmity. His sister was well known to every one as a loose character, and went off with a regiment of chasseurs which was stationed at Mirgorod five years ago; but she inscribed her husband as a peasant. His father and mother too were not law-abiding people, and both were inconceivable drunkards. The afore-mentioned nobleman and robber, Pererepenko, in his beastly and blameworthy actions, goes beyond all his family, and under the guise of piety does the most immoral things. He does not observe the fasts; for on the eve of St. Philip's this atheist bought a sheep, and next day ordered his mistress, Gapka, to kill it, alleging that he needed tallow for lamps and candles at once.

"Therefore I pray that the said nobleman, a manifest robber, church-thief, and rascal, convicted of plundering and stealing, may be put in irons, and confined in the jail or the government prison, and there, under supervision, deprived of his rank and nobility, well flogged, and banished to forced labour in Siberia, and that he may be commanded to pay damages and costs, and that judgment may be rendered on this my petition.

"To this plaint, Ivan Dovgotchkun, son of Nikifor, noble of the Mirgorod district, has set his hand."

As soon as the secretary had finished reading, Ivan Nikiforovitch seized his hat and bowed, with the intention of departing.

"Where are you going, Ivan Nikiforovitch?" the judge called after him. "Sit down a little while. Have some tea. Orishko, why are you standing there, you stupid girl, winking at the clerks? Go, bring tea."

But Ivan Nikiforovitch, in terror at having got so far from home, and at having undergone such a fearful quarantine, made haste to crawl through the door, saying, "Don't trouble yourself. It is with pleasure that I—" and closed it after him, leaving all present stupefied.

There was nothing to be done. Both plaints were entered; and the affair promised to assume a sufficiently serious aspect when an unforeseen occurrence lent an added interest to it. As the judge was leaving the court in company with the clerk and secretary, and the employees were thrusting into sacks the fowls, eggs, loaves, pies, cracknels, and other odds and ends brought by the plaintiffs—just at that moment a brown sow rushed into the room and snatched, to the amazement of the spectators, neither a pie nor a crust of bread but Ivan Nikiforovitch's plaint, which lay at the end of the table with its leaves hanging over. Having seized the document, mistress sow ran off so briskly that not one of the clerks or officials could catch her, in spite of the rulers and ink-bottles they hurled after her.

This extraordinary occurrence produced a terrible muddle, for there had not even been a copy taken of the plaint. The judge, that is to say, his secretary and the assistant debated for a long time upon such an unheard-of affair. Finally it was decided to write a report of the matter to the governor, as the investigation of the matter pertained more to the department of the city police. Report No. 389 was despatched to him that same day; and also upon that day there came to light a sufficiently curious explanation, which the reader may learn from the following chapter.

CHAPTER V

IN WHICH ARE DETAILED THE DELIBERATIONS OF TWO IMPORTANT PERSONAGES OF MIRGOROD

As soon as Ivan Ivanovitch had arranged his domestic affairs and stepped out upon the balcony, according to his custom, to lie down, he saw, to his indescribable amazement, something red at the gate. This was the red facings of the chief of police's coat, which were polished equally with his collar, and resembled varnished leather on the edges.

Ivan Ivanovitch thought to himself, "It's not bad that Peter Feodorovitch has come to talk it over with me." But he was very much surprised to see that the chief was walking remarkably fast and flourishing his hands, which was very rarely the case with him. There were eight buttons on the chief of police's uniform: the ninth, torn off in some manner during the procession at the consecration of the church two years before, the police had not been able to find up to this time: although the chief, on the occasion of the daily reports made to him by the sergeants, always asked, "Has that button been found?" These eight buttons were strewn about him as women sow beans—one to the right and one to the left. His left foot had been struck by a ball in the last campaign, and so he limped and threw it out so far to one side as to almost counteract the efforts of the right foot. The more briskly the chief of police worked his walking apparatus the less progress he made in advance. So while he was getting to the balcony, Ivan Ivanovitch had plenty of time to lose himself in surmises as to why the chief was flourishing his hands so vigorously. This interested him the more, as the matter seemed one of unusual importance; for the chief had on a new dagger.

"Good morning, Peter Feodorovitch!" cried Ivan Ivanovitch, who was, as has already been stated, exceedingly curious, and could not restrain his impatience as the chief of police began to ascend to the balcony, yet never raised his eyes, and kept grumbling at his foot, which could not be persuaded to mount the step at the first attempt.

"I wish my good friend and benefactor, Ivan Ivanovitch, a good-day," replied the chief.

"Pray sit down. I see that you are weary, as your lame foot hinders—"

"My foot!" screamed the chief, bestowing upon Ivan Ivanovitch a glance such as a giant might cast upon a pigmy, a pedant upon a dancing-master: and he stretched out his foot and stamped upon the floor with it. This boldness cost him dear; for his whole body wavered and his nose struck the railing; but the brave preserver of order, with the purpose of making light of it, righted himself immediately, and began to feel in his pocket as if to get his snuff-box. "I must report to you, my dear friend and benefactor, Ivan Ivanovitch, that never in all my days have I made such a march. Yes, seriously. For instance, during the campaign of 1807—Ah! I will tell to you how I crawled through the enclosure to see a pretty little German." Here the chief closed one eye and executed a diabolically sly smile.

"Where have you been to-day?" asked Ivan Ivanovitch, wishing to cut the chief short and bring him more speedily to the object of his visit. He would have very much liked to inquire what the chief meant to tell him, but his extensive knowledge of the world showed him the impropriety of such a question; and so he had to keep himself well in hand and await a solution, his heart, meanwhile, beating with unusual force.

"Ah, excuse me! I was going to tell you—where was I?" answered the chief of police. "In the first place, I report that the weather is fine to-day."

At these last words, Ivan Ivanovitch nearly died.

"But permit me," went on the chief. "I have come to you to-day about a very important affair." Here the chief's face and bearing assumed the same careworn aspect with which he had ascended to the balcony.

Ivan Ivanovitch breathed again, and shook as if in a fever, omitting not, as was his habit, to put a question. "What is the important matter? Is it important?"

"Pray judge for yourself; in the first place I venture to report to you, dear friend and benefactor, Ivan Ivanovitch, that you—I beg you to observe that, for my own part, I should have nothing to say; but the rules of government require it—that you have transgressed the rules of propriety."

"What do you mean, Peter Feodorovitch? I don't understand at all."

"Pardon me, Ivan Ivanovitch! how can it be that you do not understand? Your own beast has destroyed an important government document; and you can still say, after that, that you do not understand!"

"What beast?"

"Your own brown sow, with your permission, be it said."

"How can I be responsible? Why did the door-keeper of the court open the door?"

"But, Ivan Ivanovitch, your own brown sow. You must be responsible."

"I am extremely obliged to you for comparing me to a sow."

"But I did not say that, Ivan Ivanovitch! By Heaven! I did not say so! Pray judge from your own clear conscience. It is known to you without doubt, that in accordance with the views of the government, unclean animals are forbidden to roam about the town, particularly in the principal streets. Admit, now, that it is prohibited."

"God knows what you are talking about! A mighty important business that a sow got into the street!"

"Permit me to inform you, Ivan Ivanovitch, permit me, permit me, that this is utterly inadvisable. What is to be done? The authorities command, we must obey. I don't deny that sometimes chickens and geese run about the street, and even about the square, pray observe, chickens and geese; but only last year, I gave orders that pigs and goats were not to be admitted to the public squares, which regulations I directed to be read aloud at the time before all the people."

"No, Peter Feodorovitch, I see nothing here except that you are doing your best to insult me."

"But you cannot say that, my dearest friend and benefactor, that I have tried to insult you. Bethink yourself: I never said a word to you last year when you built a roof a whole foot higher than is allowed by law. On the contrary, I pretended not to have observed it. Believe me, my dearest friend, even now, I would, so to speak—but my duty—in a word, my duty demands that I should have an eye to cleanliness. Just judge for yourself, when suddenly in the principal street—"

"Fine principal streets yours are! Every woman goes there and throws down any rubbish she chooses."

"Permit me to inform you, Ivan Ivanovitch, that it is you who are insulting me. That does sometimes happen, but, as a rule, only besides fences, sheds, or storehouses; but that a filthy sow should intrude herself in the main street, in the square, now is a matter—"

"What sort of a matter? Peter Feodorovitch! surely a sow is one of God's creatures!"

"Agreed. Everybody knows that you are a learned man, that you are acquainted with sciences and various other subjects. I never studied the sciences: I began to learn to write in my thirteenth year. Of course you know that I was a soldier in the ranks."

"Hm!" said Ivan Ivanovitch.

"Yes," continued the chief of police, "in 1801 I was in the Forty-second Regiment of chasseurs, lieutenant in the fourth company. The commander of our company was, if I may be permitted to mention it, Captain Eremeeff." Thereupon the chief of police thrust his fingers into the snuff-box which Ivan Ivanovitch was holding open, and stirred up the snuff.

Ivan Ivanovitch answered, "Hm!"

"But my duty," went on the chief of police, "is to obey the commands of the authorities. Do you know, Ivan Ivanovitch, that a person who purloins a government document in the court-room incurs capital punishment equally with other criminals?"

"I know it; and, if you like, I can give you lessons. It is so decreed with regard to people, as if you, for instance, were to steal a document; but a sow is an animal, one of God's creatures."

"Certainly; but the law reads, 'Those guilty of theft'—I beg of you to listen most attentively—'Those guilty!' Here is indicated neither race nor sex nor rank: of course an animal can be guilty. You may say what you please; but the animal, until the sentence is pronounced by the court, should be committed to the charge of the police as a transgressor of the law."

"No, Peter Feodorovitch," retorted Ivan Ivanovitch coolly, "that shall not be."

"As you like: only I must carry out the orders of the authorities."

"What are you threatening me with? Probably you want to send that one-armed soldier after her. I shall order the woman who tends the door to drive him off with the poker: he'll get his last arm broken."

"I dare not dispute with you. In case you will not commit the sow to the charge of the police, then do what you please with her: kill her for Christmas, if you like, and make hams of her, or eat her as she is. Only I should like to ask you, in case you make sausages, to send me a couple, such as your Gapka makes so well, of blood and lard. My Agrafena Trofimovna is extremely fond of them."

"I will send you a couple of sausages if you permit."

"I shall be extremely obliged to you, dear friend and benefactor. Now permit me to say one word more. I am commissioned by the judge, as well as by all our acquaintances, so to speak, to effect a reconciliation between you and your friend, Ivan Nikiforovitch."

"What! with that brute! I to be reconciled to that clown! Never! It shall not be, it shall not be!" Ivan Ivanovitch was in a remarkably determined frame of mind.

"As you like," replied the chief of police, treating both nostrils to snuff. "I will not venture to advise you; but permit me to mention—here you live at enmity, and if you make peace..."

But Ivan Ivanovitch began to talk about catching quail, as he usually did when he wanted to put an end to a conversation. So the chief of police was obliged to retire without having achieved any success whatever.

CHAPTER VI

FROM WHICH THE READER CAN EASILY DISCOVER WHAT IS CONTAINED IN IT

In spite of all the judge's efforts to keep the matter secret, all Mirgorod knew by the next day that Ivan Ivanovitch's sow had stolen Ivan Nikiforovitch's petition. The chief of police himself, in a moment of forgetfulness, was the first to betray himself. When Ivan Nikiforovitch was informed of it he said nothing: he merely inquired, "Was it the brown one?"

But Agafya Fedosyevna, who was present, began again to urge on Ivan Nikiforovitch. "What's the matter with you, Ivan Nikiforovitch? People will laugh at you as at a fool if you let it pass. How can you remain a nobleman after that? You will be worse than the old woman who sells the honeycakes with hemp-seed oil you are so fond of."

And the mischief-maker persuaded him. She hunted up somewhere a middle-aged man with dark complexion, spots all over his face, and a dark-blue surtout patched on the elbows, a regular official scribbler. He blacked his boots with tar, wore three pens behind his ear, and a glass vial tied to his buttonhole with a string instead of an ink-bottle: ate as many as nine pies at once, and put the tenth in his pocket, and wrote so many slanders of all sorts on a single sheet of stamped paper that no reader could get through all at one time without interspersing coughs and sneezes. This man laboured, toiled, and wrote, and finally concocted the following document:—

"To the District Judge of Mirgorod, from the noble, Ivan Dovgotchkun, son of Nikifor.

"In pursuance of my plaint which was presented by me, Ivan Dovgotchkun, son of Nikifor, against the nobleman, Ivan Pererepenko, son of Ivan, to which the judge of the Mirgorod district court has exhibited indifference; and the shameless, high-handed deed of the brown sow being kept secret, and coming to my ears from outside parties.

"And the said neglect, plainly malicious, lies incontestably at the judge's door; for the sow is a stupid animal, and therefore unfitted for the theft of papers. From which it plainly appears that the said frequently mentioned sow was not otherwise than instigated to the same by the opponent, Ivan Pererepenko, son of Ivan, calling himself a nobleman, and already convicted of theft, conspiracy against life, and desecration of a church. But the said Mirgorod judge, with the partisanship peculiar to him, gave his private consent to this individual; for without such consent the said sow could by no possible means have been admitted to carry off the document; for the judge of the district court of Mirgorod is well provided with servants: it was only necessary to summon a soldier, who is always on duty in the reception-room, and who, although he has but one eye and one somewhat damaged arm, has powers quite adequate to driving out a sow, and to beating it with a stick, from which is credibly evident the criminal neglect of the said Mirgorod judge and the incontestable sharing of the Jew-like spoils therefrom resulting from these mutual conspirators. And the aforesaid robber and nobleman, Ivan Pererepenko, son of Ivan, having disgraced himself, finished his turning on his lathe. Wherefore, I, the noble Ivan Dovgotchkun, son of Nikifor, declare to the said district judge in proper form that if the said brown sow, or the man Pererepenko, be not summoned to the court, and judgment in accordance with justice and my advantage pronounced upon her, then I, Ivan Dovgotchkun, son of Nikifor, shall present a plaint, with observance of all due formalities, against the said district judge for his illegal partisanship to the superior courts.

"Ivan Dovgotchkun, son of Nikifor, noble of the Mirgorod District."

This petition produced its effect. The judge was a man of timid disposition, as all good people generally are. He betook himself to the secretary. But the secretary emitted from his lips a thick "Hm," and exhibited on his countenance that indifferent and diabolically equivocal expression which Satan alone assumes when he sees his victim hastening to his feet. One resource remained to him, to reconcile the two friends. But how to set about it, when all attempts up to that time had been so unsuccessful? Nevertheless, it was decided to make another effort; but Ivan Ivanovitch declared outright that he would not hear of it, and even flew into a violent passion; whilst Ivan Nikiforovitch, in lieu of an answer, turned his back and would not utter a word.

Then the case went on with the unusual promptness upon which courts usually pride themselves. Documents were dated, labelled, numbered, sewed together, registered all in one day, and the matter laid on the shelf, where it continued to lie, for one, two, or three years. Many brides were married; a new street was laid out in Mirgorod; one of the judge's double teeth fell out and two of his eye-teeth; more children than ever ran about Ivan Ivanovitch's yard; Ivan Nikiforovitch, as a reproof to Ivan Ivanovitch, constructed a new goose-shed, although a little farther back than the first, and built himself completely off from his neighbour, so that these worthy people hardly ever beheld each other's faces; but still the case lay in the cabinet, which had become marbled with ink-pots.

In the meantime a very important event for all Mirgorod had taken place. The chief of police had given a reception. Whence shall I obtain the brush and colours to depict this varied gathering and magnificent feast? Take your watch, open it, and look what is going on inside. A fearful confusion, is it not? Now, imagine almost the same, if not a greater, number of wheels standing in the chief of police's courtyard. How many carriages and waggons were there! One was wide behind and narrow in front; another narrow behind and wide in front. One was a carriage and a waggon combined; another neither a carriage nor a waggon. One resembled a huge hayrick or a fat merchant's wife; another a dilapidated Jew or a skeleton not quite freed from the skin. One was a perfect pipe with long stem in profile; another, resembling nothing whatever, suggested some strange, shapeless, fantastic object. In the midst of this chaos of wheels rose coaches with windows like those of a room. The drivers, in grey Cossack coats, gaberdines, and white hare-skin coats, sheepskin hats and caps of various patterns, and with pipes in their hands, drove the unharnessed horses through the yard.

What a reception the chief of police gave! Permit me to run through the list of those who were there: Taras Tarasovitch, Evpl Akinfovitch, Evtikhiy Evtikhievitch, Ivan Ivanovitch—not that Ivan Ivanovitch but another—Gabba Bavrilonovitch, our Ivan Ivanovitch, Elevferiy Elevferievitch, Makar Nazarevitch, Thoma Grigorovitch—I can say no more: my powers fail me, my hand stops writing. And how many ladies were there! dark and fair, tall and short, some fat like Ivan Nikiforovitch, and some so thin that it seemed as though each one might hide herself in the scabbard of the chief's sword. What head-dresses! what costumes! red, yellow, coffee-colour, green, blue, new, turned, re-made dresses, ribbons, reticules. Farewell, poor eyes! you will never be good for anything any more after such a spectacle. And how long the table was drawn out! and how all talked! and what a noise they made! What is a mill with its driving-wheel, stones, beams, hammers, wheels, in comparison with this? I cannot tell you exactly what they talked about, but presumably of many agreeable and useful things, such as the weather, dogs, wheat, caps, and dice. At length Ivan Ivanovitch—not our Ivan Ivanovitch, but the other, who had but one eye—said, "It strikes me as strange that my right eye," this one-eyed Ivan Ivanovitch always spoke sarcastically about himself, "does not see Ivan Nikiforovitch, Gospodin Dovgotchkun."

"He would not come," said the chief of police.

"Why not?"

"It's two years now, glory to God! since they quarrelled; that is, Ivan Ivanovitch and Ivan Nikiforovitch; and where one goes, the other will not go."

"You don't say so!" Thereupon one-eyed Ivan Ivanovitch raised his eye and clasped his hands. "Well, if people with good eyes cannot live in peace, how am I to live amicably, with my bad one?"

At these words they all laughed at the tops of their voices. Every one liked one-eyed Ivan Ivanovitch, because he cracked jokes in that style. A tall, thin man in a frieze coat, with a plaster on his nose, who up to this time had sat in the corner, and never once altered the expression of his face, even when a fly lighted on his nose, rose from his seat, and approached nearer to the crowd which surrounded one-eyed Ivan Ivanovitch. "Listen," said Ivan Ivanovitch, when he perceived that quite a throng had collected about him; "suppose we make peace between our friends. Ivan Ivanovitch is talking with the women and girls; let us send quietly for Ivan Nikiforovitch and bring them together."

Ivan Ivanovitch's proposal was unanimously agreed to; and it was decided to send at once to Ivan Nikiforovitch's house, and beg him, at any rate, to come to the chief of police's for dinner. But the difficult question as to who was to be intrusted with this weighty commission rendered all thoughtful. They debated long as to who was the most expert in diplomatic matters. At length it was unanimously agreed to depute Anton Prokofievitch to do this business.

But it is necessary, first of all, to make the reader somewhat acquainted with this noteworthy person. Anton Prokofievitch was a truly good man, in the fullest meaning of the term. If any one in Mirgorod gave him a neckerchief or underclothes, he returned thanks; if any one gave him a fillip on the nose, he returned thanks too. If he was asked, "Why, Anton Prokofievitch, do you wear a light brown coat with blue sleeves?" he generally replied, "Ah, you haven't one like it! Wait a bit, it will soon fade and will be alike all over." And, in point of fact, the blue cloth, from the effects of the sun, began to turn cinnamon colour, and became of the same tint as the rest of the coat. But the strange part of it was that Anton Prokofievitch had a habit of wearing woollen clothing in summer and nankeen in winter.

Anton Prokofievitch had no house of his own. He used to have one on the outskirts of the town; but he sold it, and with the purchase-money bought a team of brown horses and a little carriage in which he drove about to stay with the squires. But as the horses were a deal of trouble and money was required for oats, Anton Prokofievitch bartered them for a violin and a housemaid, with twenty-five paper rubles to boot. Afterwards Anton Prokofievitch sold the violin, and exchanged the girl for a morocco and gold tobacco-pouch; now he has such a tobacco-pouch as no one else has. As a result of this luxury, he can no longer go about among the country houses, but has to remain in the town and pass the night at different houses, especially of those gentlemen who take pleasure in tapping him on the nose. Anton Prokofievitch is very fond of good eating, and plays a good game at cards. Obeying orders always was his forte; so, taking his hat and cane, he set out at once on his errand.

But, as he walked along, he began to ponder in what manner he should contrive to induce Ivan Nikiforovitch to come to the assembly. The unbending character of the latter, who was otherwise a worthy man, rendered the undertaking almost hopeless. How, indeed, was he to persuade him to come, when even rising from his bed cost him so great an effort? But supposing that he did rise, how could he get him to come, where, as he doubtless knew, his irreconcilable enemy already was? The more Anton Prokofievitch reflected, the more difficulties he perceived. The day was sultry, the sun beat down, the perspiration poured from him in streams. Anton Prokofievitch was a tolerably sharp man in many respects though they did tap him on the nose. In bartering, however, he was not fortunate. He knew very well when to play the fool, and sometimes contrived to turn things to his own profit amid circumstances and surroundings from which a wise man could rarely escape without loss.

His ingenious mind had contrived a means of persuading Ivan Nikiforovitch; and he was proceeding bravely to face everything when an unexpected occurrence somewhat disturbed his equanimity. There is no harm, at this point, in admitting to the reader that, among other things, Anton Prokofievitch was the owner of a pair of trousers of such singular properties that whenever he put them on the dogs always bit his calves. Unfortunately, he had donned this particular pair of trousers; and he had hardly given himself up to meditation before a fearful barking on all sides saluted his ears. Anton Prokofievitch raised such a yell, no one could scream louder than he, that not only did the well-known woman and the occupant of the endless coat rush out to meet him, but even the small boys from Ivan Ivanovitch's yard. But although the dogs succeeded in tasting only one of his calves, this sensibility diminished his courage, and he entered the porch with a certain amount of timidity.

CHAPTER VII

HOW A RECONCILIATION WAS SOUGHT TO BE EFFECTED AND A LAW SUIT ENSUED

"Ah! how do you do? Why do you irritate the dogs?" said Ivan Nikiforovitch, on perceiving Anton Prokofievitch; for no one spoke otherwise than jestingly with Anton Prokofievitch.

"Hang them! who's been irritating them?" retorted Anton Prokofievitch.

"You have!"

"By Heavens, no! You are invited to dinner by Peter Feodorovitch."

"Hm!"

"He invited you in a more pressing manner than I can tell you. 'Why,' says he, 'does Ivan Nikiforovitch shun me like an enemy? He never comes round to have a chat, or make a call.'"

Ivan Nikiforovitch stroked his beard.

"'If,' says he, 'Ivan Nikiforovitch does not come now, I shall not know what to think: surely, he must have some design against me. Pray, Anton Prokofievitch, persuade Ivan

Nikiforovitch!' Come, Ivan Nikiforovitch, let us go! a very choice company is already met there."

Ivan Nikiforovitch began to look at a cock, which was perched on the roof, crowing with all its might.

"If you only knew, Ivan Nikiforovitch," pursued the zealous ambassador, "what fresh sturgeon and caviare Peter Feodorovitch has had sent to him!" Whereupon Ivan Nikiforovitch turned his head and began to listen attentively. This encouraged the messenger. "Come quickly: Thoma Grigorovitch is there too. Why don't you come?" he added, seeing that Ivan Nikiforovitch still lay in the same position. "Shall we go, or not?"

"I won't!"

This "I won't" startled Anton Prokofievitch. He had fancied that his alluring representations had quite moved this very worthy man; but instead, he heard that decisive "I won't."

"Why won't you?" he asked, with a vexation which he very rarely exhibited, even when they put burning paper on his head, a trick which the judge and the chief of police were particularly fond of indulging in.

Ivan Nikiforovitch took a pinch of snuff.

"Just as you like, Ivan Nikiforovitch. I do not know what detains you."

"Why don't I go?" said Ivan Nikiforovitch at length: "because that brigand will be there!" This was his ordinary way of alluding to Ivan Ivanovitch. "Just God! and is it long?"

"He will not be there, he will not be there! May the lightning kill me on the spot!" returned Anton Prokofievitch, who was ready to perjure himself ten times in an hour. "Come along, Ivan Nikiforovitch!"

"You lie, Anton Prokofievitch! he is there!"

"By Heaven, by Heaven, he's not! May I never stir from this place if he's there! Now, just think for yourself, what object have I in lying? May my hands and feet wither!— What, don't you believe me now? May I perish right here in your presence! Don't you believe me yet?"

Ivan Nikiforovitch was entirely reassured by these asseverations, and ordered his valet, in the boundless coat, to fetch his trousers and nankeen spencer.

To describe how Ivan Nikiforovitch put on his trousers, how they wound his neckerchief about his neck, and finally dragged on his spencer, which burst under the left sleeve, would be quite superfluous. Suffice it to say, that during the whole of the time he preserved a becoming calmness of demeanour, and answered not a word to Anton Prokofievitch's proposition to exchange something for his Turkish tobacco-pouch.

Meanwhile, the assembly awaited with impatience the decisive moment when Ivan Nikiforovitch should make his appearance and at length comply with the general desire that these worthy people should be reconciled to each other. Many were almost convinced that Ivan Nikiforovitch would not come. Even the chief of police offered to bet with one-eyed Ivan Ivanovitch that he would not come; and only desisted when one-eyed Ivan Ivanovitch demanded that he should wager his lame foot against his own bad eye, at which the chief of police was greatly offended, and the company enjoyed a quiet laugh. No one had yet sat down to the table, although it was long past two o'clock, an hour before which in Mirgorod, even on ceremonial occasions, every one had already dined.

No sooner did Anton Prokofievitch show himself in the doorway, then he was instantly surrounded. Anton Prokofievitch, in answer to all inquiries, shouted the all-decisive words, "He will not come!" No sooner had he uttered them than a hailstorm of reproaches, scoldings, and, possibly, even fillips were about to descend upon his head for the ill success of his mission, when all at once the door opened, and—Ivan Nikiforovitch entered.

If Satan himself or a corpse had appeared, it would not have caused such consternation amongst the company as Ivan Nikiforovitch's unexpected arrival created. But Anton Prokofievitch only went off into a fit of laughter, and held his sides with delight at having played such a joke upon the company.

At all events, it was almost past the belief of all that Ivan Nikiforovitch could, in so brief a space of time, have attired himself like a respectable gentleman. Ivan Ivanovitch was not there at the moment: he had stepped out somewhere. Recovering from their amazement, the guests expressed an interest in Ivan Nikiforovitch's health, and their pleasure at his increase in breadth. Ivan Nikiforovitch kissed every one, and said, "Very much obliged!"

Meantime, the fragrance of the beet-soup was wafted through the apartment, and tickled the nostrils of the hungry guests very agreeably. All rushed headlong to table. The line of ladies, loquacious and silent, thin and stout, swept on, and the long table soon glittered with all the hues of the rainbow. I will not describe the courses: I will make no mention of the curd dumplings with sour cream, nor of the dish of pig's fry that was served with the soup, nor of the turkey with plums and raisins, nor of the dish which greatly resembled in appearance a boot soaked in kvas, nor of the sauce, which is the swan's song of the old-fashioned cook, nor of that other dish which was brought in all enveloped in the flames of spirit, and amused as well as frightened the ladies extremely. I will say nothing of these dishes, because I like to eat them better than to spend many words in discussing them.

Ivan Ivanovitch was exceedingly pleased with the fish dressed with horse-radish. He devoted himself especially to this useful and nourishing preparation. Picking out all the fine bones from the fish, he laid them on his plate; and happening to glance across the table—Heavenly Creator; but this was strange! Opposite him sat Ivan Nikiforovitch.

At the very same instant Ivan Nikiforovitch glanced up also—No, I can do no more—Give me a fresh pen with a fine point for this picture! mine is flabby. Their faces seemed to turn to stone whilst still retaining their defiant expression. Each beheld a long familiar face, to which it should have seemed the most natural of things to step up, involuntarily, as to an unexpected friend, and offer a snuff-box, with the words, "Do me the favour," or "Dare I beg you to do me the favour?" Instead of this, that face was terrible as a forerunner of evil. The perspiration poured in streams from Ivan Ivanovitch and Ivan Nikiforovitch.

All the guests at the table grew dumb with attention, and never once took their eyes off the former friends. The ladies, who had been busy up to that time on a sufficiently interesting discussion as to the preparation of capons, suddenly cut their conversation short. All was silence. It was a picture worthy of the brush of a great artist.

At length Ivan Ivanovitch pulled out his handkerchief and began to blow his nose; whilst Ivan Nikiforovitch glanced about and his eye rested on the open door. The chief of police at once perceived this movement, and ordered the door to be fastened. Then both of the friends began to eat, and never once glanced at each other again.

As soon as dinner was over, the two former friends both rose from their seats, and began to look for their hats, with a view to departure. Then the chief beckoned; and Ivan Ivanovitch—not our Ivan Ivanovitch, but the other with the one eye—got behind Ivan Nikiforovitch, and the chief stepped behind Ivan Ivanovitch, and the two began to drag them backwards, in order to bring them together, and not release them till they had shaken hands with each other. Ivan Ivanovitch, the one-eyed, pushed Ivan Nikiforovitch, with tolerable success, towards the spot where stood Ivan Ivanovitch. But the chief of police directed his course too much to one side, because he could not steer himself with his refractory leg, which obeyed no orders whatever on this occasion, and, as if with malice and aforethought, swung itself uncommonly far, and in quite the contrary direction, possibly from the fact that there had been an unusual amount of fruit wine after dinner, so that Ivan Ivanovitch fell over a lady in a red gown, who had thrust herself into the very midst, out of curiosity.

Such an omen forboded no good. Nevertheless, the judge, in order to set things to rights, took the chief of police's place, and, sweeping all the snuff from his upper lip with his nose, pushed Ivan Ivanovitch in the opposite direction. In Mirgorod this is the usual manner of effecting a reconciliation: it somewhat resembles a game of ball. As soon as the judge pushed Ivan Ivanovitch, Ivan Ivanovitch with the one eye exerted all his strength, and pushed Ivan Nikiforovitch, from whom the perspiration streamed like rain-water from a roof. In spite of the fact that the friends resisted to the best of their ability, they were nevertheless brought together, for the two chief movers received reinforcements from the ranks of their guests.

Then they were closely surrounded on all sides, not to be released until they had decided to give one another their hands. "God be with you, Ivan Nikiforovitch and Ivan Ivanovitch! declare upon your honour now, that what you quarrelled about were mere trifles, were they not? Are you not ashamed of yourselves before people and before God?"

"I do not know," said Ivan Nikiforovitch, panting with fatigue, though it is to be observed that he was not at all disinclined to a reconciliation, "I do not know what I did to Ivan Ivanovitch; but why did he destroy my coop and plot against my life?"

"I am innocent of any evil designs!" said Ivan Ivanovitch, never looking at Ivan Nikiforovitch. "I swear before God and before you, honourable noblemen, I did nothing to my enemy! Why does he calumniate me and insult my rank and family?"

"How have I insulted you, Ivan Ivanovitch?" said Ivan Nikiforovitch. One moment more of explanation, and the long enmity would have been extinguished. Ivan

Nikiforovitch was already feeling in his pocket for his snuff-box, and was about to say, "Do me the favour."

"Is it not an insult," answered Ivan Ivanovitch, without raising his eyes, "when you, my dear sir, insulted my honour and my family with a word which it is improper to repeat here?"

"Permit me to observe, in a friendly manner, Ivan Ivanovitch," here Ivan Nikiforovitch touched Ivan Ivanovitch's button with his finger, which clearly indicated the disposition of his mind, "that you took offence, the deuce only knows at what, because I called you a 'goose'—"

It occurred to Ivan Nikiforovitch that he had made a mistake in uttering that word; but it was too late: the word was said. Everything went to the winds. It, on the utterance of this word without witnesses, Ivan Ivanovitch lost control of himself and flew into such a passion as God preserve us from beholding any man in, what was to be expected now? I put it to you, dear readers, what was to be expected now, when the fatal word was uttered in an assemblage of persons among whom were ladies, in whose presence Ivan Ivanovitch liked to be particularly polite? If Ivan Nikiforovitch had set to work in any other manner, if he had only said bird and not goose, it might still have been arranged, but all was at an end.

He gave one look at Ivan Nikiforovitch, but such a look! If that look had possessed active power, then it would have

turned Ivan Nikiforovitch into dust. The guests understood
the look and hastened to separate them. And this man, the
very model of gentleness, who never let a single poor woman
go by without interrogating her, rushed out in a fearful rage.
Such violent storms do passions produce!

For a whole month nothing was heard of Ivan Ivanovitch.
He shut himself up at home. His ancestral chest was opened,
and from it were taken silver rubles, his grandfather's old
silver rubles! And these rubles passed into the ink-stained
hands of legal advisers. The case was sent up to the higher
court; and when Ivan Ivanovitch received the joyful news
that it would be decided on the morrow, then only did he
look out upon the world and resolve to emerge from his
house. Alas! from that time forth the council gave notice day
by day that the case would be finished on the morrow, for
the space of ten years.

Five years ago, I passed through the town of Mirgorod. I
came at a bad time. It was autumn, with its damp, melancholy
weather, mud and mists. An unnatural verdure, the result of
incessant rains, covered with a watery network the fields and
meadows, to which it is as well suited as youthful pranks to
an old man, or roses to an old woman. The weather made
a deep impression on me at the time: when it was dull, I
was dull; but in spite of this, when I came to pass through
Mirgorod, my heart beat violently. God, what reminiscences!
I had not seen Mirgorod for twenty years. Here had lived, in

touching friendship, two inseparable friends. And how many prominent people had died! Judge Demyan Demyanovitch was already gone: Ivan Ivanovitch, with the one eye, had long ceased to live.

I entered the main street. All about stood poles with bundles of straw on top: some alterations were in progress. Several dwellings had been removed. The remnants of board and wattled fences projected sadly here and there. It was a festival day. I ordered my basket chaise to stop in front of the church, and entered softly that no one might turn round. To tell the truth, there was no need of this: the church was almost empty; there were very few people; it was evident that even the most pious feared the mud. The candles seemed strangely unpleasant in that gloomy, or rather sickly, light. The dim vestibule was melancholy; the long windows, with their circular panes, were bedewed with tears of rain. I retired into the vestibule, and addressing a respectable old man, with greyish hair, said, "May I inquire if Ivan Nikiforovitch is still living?"

At that moment the lamp before the holy picture burned up more brightly and the light fell directly upon the face of my companion. What was my surprise, on looking more closely, to behold features with which I was acquainted! It was Ivan Nikiforovitch himself! But how he had changed!

"Are you well, Ivan Nikiforovitch? How old you have grown!"

"Yes, I have grown old. I have just come from Poltava to-day," answered Ivan Nikiforovitch.

"You don't say so! you have been to Poltava in such bad weather?"

"What was to be done? that lawsuit—"

At this I sighed involuntarily.

Ivan Nikiforovitch observed my sigh, and said, "Do not be troubled: I have reliable information that the case will be decided next week, and in my favour."

I shrugged my shoulders, and went to seek news of Ivan Ivanovitch.

"Ivan Ivanovitch is here," some one said to me, "in the choir."

I saw a gaunt form. Was that Ivan Ivanovitch? His face was covered with wrinkles, his hair was perfectly white; but the pelisse was the same as ever. After the first greetings were over, Ivan Ivanovitch, turning to me with a joyful smile which always became his funnel-shaped face, said, "Have you been told the good news?"

"What news?" I inquired.

"My case is to be decided to-morrow without fail: the court has announced it decisively."

I sighed more deeply than before, made haste to take my leave, for I was bound on very important business, and seated myself in my kibitka.

The lean nags known in Mirgorod as post-horses started, producing with their hoofs, which were buried in a grey mass of mud, a sound very displeasing to the ear. The rain poured in torrents upon the Jew seated on the box, covered with a rug. The dampness penetrated through and through me. The gloomy barrier with a sentry-box, in which an old soldier was repairing his weapons, was passed slowly. Again the same fields, in some places black where they had been dug up, in others of a greenish hue; wet daws and crows; monotonous rain; a tearful sky, without one gleam of light!... It is gloomy in this world, gentlemen!